To all the babies and dogs who have made my life so sweet. – LEM

For my sausage dog and his mum. – GA

Text copyright © 2017 by Linda Elovitz Marshall
Illustrations copyright © 2017 by Ged Adamson

First edition 2017
Published by Peter Pauper Press, Inc.
202 Mamaroneck Avenue
White Plains, New York 10601 USA

Published in the United Kingdom and Europe by Peter Pauper Press, Inc.
c/o White Pebble International
Unit 2, Plot 11 Terminus Rd.
Chichester, West Sussex PO19 8TX, UK

Library of Congress Cataloging-in-Publication Data Available

ISBN 978-1-4413-2238-8
Manufactured for Peter Pauper Press, Inc.
Printed in Hong Kong

7 6 5 4 3 2 1

Visit us at www.peterpauper.com

MOMMY, BABY, AND ME

By Linda Elovitz Marshall

Illustrated by Ged Adamson

PETER PAUPER PRESS, INC.
White Plains, New York

A long time ago,
it was just Mommy and me.

We were very good friends.

We did everything together.
Played fetch.
Went for walks.

Cuddled. Groomed.

I sat in Mommy's lap.

I licked her hand.

She brushed my fur.

It was very nice.

Then Mommy met Daddy.

Things changed.

When Mommy and I took walks,
Daddy came, too.

Mommy and Daddy
became very good friends.

They cuddled. *A lot.*

And I got my very own bed.

Then things changed
even more.

Everything was different.

Even Mommy's lap.

It got smaller . . .

. . . and smaller.

Mommy asked if I could feel the baby kick.

Of course I could feel it kick.

It was kicking me . . .

right . . . out . . .

of her lap!

Soon, there was no room for me.

There was only room for Baby.

Mommy and Baby became very good friends.

They cuddled.

They sang.

And Mommy groomed Baby a lot.

When I wagged my tail near Baby's cradle,
Mommy yelled at *ME*!

Things were starting to be not so nice.

Everyone said, "How cute!"

Not me.

I thought Baby made *way*
too much noise,

was *way* too stinky,

and was not *at all* housebroken!

Mommy and Daddy weren't even *trying* to train Baby.

One day, Mommy and Baby
sat near a mirror. I sat near them.

I looked in the mirror.
Then I looked at Mommy and Baby.

That's when I saw it:

Baby looked a *lot* more like Mommy than I did.

Baby had two arms, two legs, and hardly any fur . . .

. . . just like Mommy.

That night, I looked at the stars and wished
things could be the way they used to be.

Things began to change.
Again.

Baby started moving
on all fours.

Like me.

Mommy and Daddy smiled.

Funny . . . I got the idea they wanted *me* to train Baby.

I started doing "big dog" things . . .

like guarding the door
while Baby slept . . .

. . . and sitting by the high chair while Baby fed me.

Things were starting to be nice again!

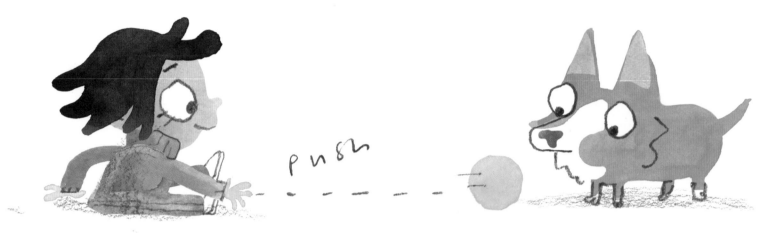

One day, Baby rolled a ball.

I fetched.

Baby rolled it again.

I fetched again.

Then Baby leaned on my back and hugged me.

NOW I know why Mommy and Daddy got Baby.

They got Baby . . . for *me*!